SKYLARK CHOOSE YOUR OWN ADVENTURE® · 3

"I DON'T LIKE CHOOSE YOUR OWN ADVENTURE® BOOKS. I *LOVE* THEM!" says Jessica Gordon, age 10. And now, kids between the ages of six and nine can choose their own adventure, too. Here's what kids have to say about the new Skylark Choose Your Own Adventure® books.

"These are my favorite books because you can pick whatever choice you want —and the story is all about you."

—Katy Alson, *age 8*

"I love finding out how my story will end."

—Joss Williams, *age 9*

"I like all the illustrations!"

—Sarritri Brightfield, *age 7*

"A six-year-old friend and I have lots of fun making the decisions together."

—Peggy Marcus *(adult)*

Bantam Books in the Choose Your Own Adventure® Series
Ask your bookseller for the books you have missed.

Choose Your Own Adventure Books for younger readers

SUNKEN TREASURE

EDWARD PACKARD

ILLUSTRATED BY PAUL GRANGER

A BANTAM SKYLARK BOOK®
TORONTO · NEW YORK · LONDON · SYDNEY

RL 2, 007-009

SUNKEN TREASURE

A Bantam Skylark® Book / April 1982
2nd printing . . . August 1982
3rd printing . . . December 1982

Published simultaneously in hardcover and Skylark®

CHOOSE YOUR OWN ADVENTURE®
is a registered trademark of Bantam Books, Inc.

Original conception of Edward Packard

Skylark Books is a registered trademark of Bantam Books, Inc.,
Registered in U.S. Patent and Trademark Office and elsewhere.

Illustrated by Paul Granger

Library of Congress Cataloging in Publication Data

Packard, Edward
Sunken treasure.

(Choose your own adventure ; 3)
Summary: The reader is asked to make choices which will
determine the outcome of a search for sunken treasure.
[1. Buried treasure—Fiction. 2. Literary recreations]
I. Granger, Paul, ill. II. Title. III. Series.
PZ7.P1245Sυ   [E]   81-20554
ISBN 0-553-05018-4   AACR2
ISBN 0-553-15208-4 (pbk.)

Published simultaneously in the United States and Canada

Bantam Books are published by Bantam Books, Inc. Its trademark, consisting of the words "Bantam Books" and the por-
trayal of a rooster, is Registered in U.S. Patent and Trademark
Office and in other countries, Marca Registrada. Bantam
Books, Inc., 666 Fifth Avenue, New York, New York 10103.

PRINTED IN THE UNITED STATES OF AMERICA

0 9 8 7 6 5

For Andrea
—with appreciation

READ THIS FIRST!!!

Most books are about other people.
This book is about you!
What happens to you depends on what you decide to do.

Do not read this book from the first page through to the last page. Instead, start on page one and read until you come to your first choice. Then turn to the page shown and see what happens.

When you come to the end of a story, go back and start again. Every choice leads to a new adventure.

Are you ready to go sailing for sunken treasure? Then turn to page one . . . and *good luck!*

Imagine . . . It's the year 1793. You live in **1** a small house in Boston. From your window you can look out at the tall ships as they sail in and out of the harbor. Your neighbor, Captain Frye, owns a schooner—the *Eagle*. His son Nick is a friend of yours. You and Nick like to listen to Captain Frye tell stories of the sea—of whales and storms and pirates.

One day, you find a box full of old letters in the attic.

Turn to page 2.

2   Among the letters is a yellowed map that looks like this:

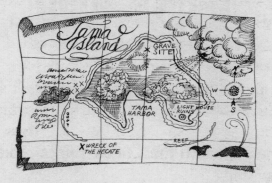

Could it be a treasure map?

"The *Eagle* is due back in port in a few days," says your father. "Captain Frye might know something about the map."

You decide to ask Captain Frye when he returns, but then you think—why wait? You could walk down to the docks right now and ask one of the sailors.

If you wait for Captain Frye to return, turn to page 4.

If you walk down to the docks to ask a sailor, turn to page 3.

You walk down to the harbor with the map. **3**
Dozens of ships are tied up to the docks. You
notice a square-rigger flying the Spanish flag.
On the stern in gold letters is its name—
Caliban. A young sailor walks by.

You hold out your map and ask, "Have
you ever heard of Tama Island?"

He studies the map for a moment and
shakes his head. "I can't read, myself, but
come on board the *Caliban.* Our captain will
know."

Turn to page 8.

4   You decide to wait for Captain Frye.

A few days later you see the *Eagle* sailing into the harbor. You run down to the dock so you can show Captain Frye the map when he steps off his ship.

His eyes light up. "This map shows the wreck of the *Hecate*," he says. "It was owned by Blue Beard the pirate. It sank in a storm fifty years ago—loaded with treasure. By Jove, I'd like to search for it!"

"Will you take me along?" you ask.

"I'd be glad to," says the Captain. "But I must warn you—Red Eye the pirate sails in those waters."

"I'm not afraid."

The Captain strokes his gray beard. "Then if your parents will let you," he says, "you and I will go sailing for sunken treasure!"

Turn to page 6.

6 Your parents have said *yes!*

You've been at sea for three weeks. Now you are standing on the deck of the *Eagle* with Captain Frye and Nick. Mr. Pym, the first mate, is steering.

The Captain hands you his brass telescope. "There's Tama Island," he says.

Turn to page 14.

The Navy ships pass by before you can signal them. They must have been fooled by the *Caliban*'s Spanish flag.

That afternoon you are cleaning the cabin when you hear the pirates shouting. You run up on deck. Standing next to the helmsman, you see Captain Frye's ship, the *Eagle*, only a few hundred yards away!

"Man the cannon!" yells Red Eye. "We'll blow that ship to bits."

The lookout yells, "There's a reef just off the port bow! Hold this course—there's deep water ahead!"

The helmsman leans over the rail to look at the reef. If you could grab the wheel from him, you could run the *Caliban* aground on the reef!

If you grab the wheel away from the helmsman, turn to page 28.

If you decide not to risk it, turn to page 17.

8   When you step aboard the ship, you are met by a man with the strangest eyes you've ever seen. One eye is brown, and the other is as red as blood.

"What brings you on my ship, my young friend?" He snatches the map out of your hand before you can answer. Then, with a cruel smile, he says, "Take our guest to the forward cabin *and lock it!*"

You try to run, but the sailor holds your arms tightly. "Don't feel bad," he says. "It's an honor to sail with Red Eye the pirate!"

Turn to page 20.

turn to page 20

The Captain and Nick row the whaleboat toward the shore, and you and Mr. Pym sail the skiff to the reef. Looking down through the water, you see dozens of blue and yellow fish. They dart under a ledge, chased by a big green fish. Beyond the ledge you see a large, dark shape.

Go on to page 11.

"I think I see the wreck!" you cry.

"And I see another ship!" Mr. Pym points to a square-rigger sailing toward the harbor. Its topsails are crimson and gold, and the pirate flag—a skull and crossbones—flies from its mast.

"It's the *Caliban*—Red Eye's ship! I've got to get back to the *Eagle*!" Mr. Pym shouts.

He quickly swings the skiff around. When you reach the *Eagle*, Mr. Pym says, "I'll try to keep those pirates from coming aboard. You'd better hide, unless you want to try to sail the skiff to shore."

If you try to sail the skiff to shore, turn to page 18.

If you hide in the sail locker, turn to page 19.

12 "I'll go ashore with Nick," you say.

"Then get into the whaleboat," says Captain Frye. "Mr. Pym and I will sail to the reef."

You climb into the stern of the boat. Nick rows toward shore with strong, swift strokes. At last the boat rises on the crest of a wave and glides up onto the beach. You jump out and help pull it on shore.

"Why don't you look for the lighthouse ruins that are shown on the map?" says Nick. "I'll climb to the top of the hill and see if I can find the grave site."

Turn to page 23.

You look at the palm groves and the long, curving beach covered with pink and white shells.

"We're close enough to anchor," says the Captain. *"Hard-a-lee!"*

Mr. Pym turns the wheel. The ship heads into the wind. Captain Frye lets the anchor over the side. You and Nick lower the sails.

The Captain says, "Mr. Pym, you take the sailing skiff and explore the reef. If our map is right, you may find the wreck of the *Hecate*! Nick, take the whaleboat in to the beach and

look for clues. For all we know, Blue Beard might have hidden his treasure ashore!"

Captain Frye asks you, "Would you rather explore the reef with Mr. Pym, or land on the island with Nick?"

If you decide to explore the reef, turn to page 10.

If you decide to go ashore, turn to page 12.

You decide not to risk grounding the *Caliban.*

"All right, lads," shouts Red Eye. *"Fire!"*

The pirates light the cannon fuse. With a great roar a cannonball goes flying toward the *Eagle.* It brings down a mast and sail. The next cannonball lands squarely on the quarter-deck.

Red Eye's cannon fires again and again. As the smoke clears you can see that the *Eagle* is sinking. But Captain Frye and his crew have gotten into the sailing skiff! They are heading toward Tama Island!

It is getting too dark to give chase. The pirates anchor the ship. You turn in for the night, but you are kept awake by the pirates' shouting on the deck overhead. Suddenly you hear the *clank, clank* of swords clashing.

Turn to page 30.

18

You jump into the skiff to escape the pirates. Mr. Pym casts you free. You start sailing toward the island, but the wind begins to change. Soon it's blowing you away from shore. You don't know how to sail against the wind, and your boat drifts rapidly out to sea. In a few hours you are almost out of sight of land.

Finally night falls. You lie down to rest, and the motion of the waves lulls you to sleep.

Turn to page 26.

You crawl into the sail locker. Then you **19** wait, listening. Soon you hear men shouting on the deck above you. The pirates must have climbed aboard!

You hear a splash. "Help!" It's Mr. Pym!

For a few moments all is quiet. Then you hear loud voices.

"The fool thinks he can swim to shore. He'll be lucky if the sharks don't eat him for dinner."

The pirates must have thrown Mr. Pym over the side!

Turn to page 34.

You are held prisoner on the *Caliban* for three weeks. When you're not up in the crow's-nest serving as lookout, you have to scrub the decks and polish the brass. At night you lie in your tiny berth and wonder if you'll ever see land again.

The sailors have told you that Red Eye has been looking for Blue Beard's treasure for a long time, and that he plans to use your map to find it.

One morning you spot two armed Navy schooners on the horizon. They are flying American flags.

If you do nothing,
turn to page 7.

If you try to get in
good with the pirates
by warning them
about the Navy ships,
turn to page 33.

Following your map, you walk east across **23** the sand dunes. Your legs feel wobbly from having been at sea so long. Suddenly you stumble into a hole. Then you see that it is not a hole, but the entrance to a tunnel!

Looking up, you see that a square-rigged ship with red and gold topsails is sailing toward the island. You cannot tell whether it is a pirate ship or not.

If you run to tell Nick about the ship, turn to page 29.

If you take time to explore the tunnel, turn to page 39.

24   Nick follows you back into the cave, and you both stare at the wooden chest.

"Are you afraid of Blue Beard's curse?" says Nick.

"I don't think so," you say. You take a sharp rock and pry open the lid. The chest is filled with gold and silver coins!

"Hurrah!" cries Nick. "Let's get back to the *Eagle* and tell the others."

Go on to page 25.

You and Nick run toward the beach. But
you see that the *Eagle* has already set sail,
followed by a square-rigged ship!

Nick grabs your arm. "It's Red Eye the pirate. I know his ship—the *Caliban!*"

You see a puff of smoke and then hear the
thunderous roar of a cannon. The *Eagle* turns
sharply toward shore. Suddenly the square-
rigger turns the other way.

"The water is too shallow for the *Caliban*,"
says Nick. "The *Eagle* is safe for now. But the
pirates are sure to come ashore."

If you say, "Let's hide in the cave,"
turn to page 48.

If you say, "Let's hide in the woods,"
turn to page 41.

26 You drift in the skiff all night. Soon it is morning, and you wake up, startled. You hear voices nearby! A three-masted ship has pulled alongside your skiff. Friendly sailors help you aboard. The captain steps up and shakes your hand. He takes you to a cabin and sets out fresh oranges and chocolate.

"I'm Captain Scarlatti and this is the *Pelican*," he says. "We are searching for Red Eye the pirate. There is a reward for his capture."

"Red Eye is at Tama Island!" you say. "I am worried about my friends there—on board the *Eagle*."

"Red Eye's the meanest pirate on the sea," says the captain. "But he'll give up—we have a cannon that can sink his ship from half a mile!"

Captain Scarlatti calls to his crew. "Set course for Tama Island. We'll free all good people, and banish Red Eye from the sea!"

The End

28   You grab the *Caliban*'s wheel with both hands and swing it to the left with all your might. The ship begins to turn.

CRUNCH! You are thrown as the *Caliban* crashes into the reef. The ship lurches sharply. Everyone yells. Red Eye goes flying across the deck. The cook pokes his head up through a hatch. *"The water's pouring in, mates. We're done for!"*

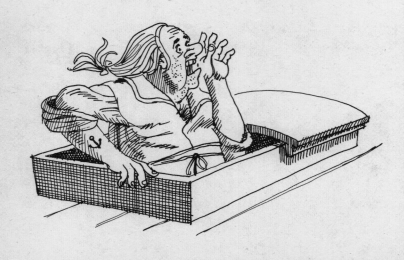

Turn to page 50.

You run to tell Nick about the ship sailing toward you. Suddenly the ground gives way. You are sliding down a steep slope until . . . *Thud!*

You land at the bottom of a pit. The sides look too steep to climb, except for one. But you have to cross a pond to get to it. You start to wade into the water, but you see three crocodiles in the pond. You leap back up against the side!

You are trapped with nothing to do but wait. The sun climbs higher. You get hot and very thirsty.

Turn to page 36.

"This is mutiny!" you hear Red Eye shout. Again the clashing of swords. And a loud splash!

You run up in time to see Red Eye crumple to the deck. "They won't tangle with me again." His voice is hoarse and weak. "They're over the side—at the bottom of the deep . . ." Those are his last words.

Looking toward the island, you see your friends sailing toward you in the *Eagle*'s skiff! In

a few minutes they are alongside the *Caliban*. They climb aboard.

"We could hear them yelling all the way from the beach," says Nick.

"How strange is fate," says Mr. Pym. "They sank our ship and gave us theirs."

Captain Frye smiles and says, "Let us be the first *good* pirates to sail the seas!"

The End

"Look ahead!" you cry to the pirates. *"Navy* **33** *ships with cannons!"*

"Bring 'er about!" Red Eye shouts.

You hang onto the mast as the sails flap in the wind. Slowly the *Caliban* swings round and heads the other way.

"Come on down!" Red Eye yells.

"You're going to make a good pirate," he says when you reach the deck. "And I have good news for you. We plan to capture the *Isabella* when she sails from Kingston. You'll have a share in the loot!"

Turn to page 46.

34   Suddenly the door swings open. A hand reaches in and pulls you out on deck. The hand belongs to a man with a broad, flat face and the strangest eyes you have ever seen. One eye is brown, and the other is as red as blood. There's no doubt who it is—Red Eye the pirate!

Two pirates stand behind him. One of them draws a dagger and holds it to your throat. But Red Eye raises his hand. He stares at you a moment, and a smile flickers across his face. "I'll take you to my ship, the *Caliban!*" he says.

"Why would you do that?" you ask.

"To make a pirate of you!"

Turn to page 20.

36   A while later, you see one of the crocodiles climbing out of the pond. It crawls slowly, step by step, along the side of the pit and stops only a few feet away.

You are afraid to move. The crocodile's huge jaws are half open. *If only you dared to step on its back—you'd be tall enough to climb out of the pit!*

The crocodile slowly lifts its head and stares at you. It's going to charge.

You've got to act fast!

If you try to step on the crocodile's back and climb out of the pit, turn to page 52.

If you throw sand in its eyes, turn to page 44.

You start to crawl through the tunnel in the sand. You have gone only a few feet when sand begins to stream down from above. Suddenly the floor of the tunnel gives way, and you fall onto the floor of a cave below!

You pick yourself up and look around. Then you shrink back in horror.

Turn to page 40.

The floor of the cave is strewn with broken bones—and two skulls. There is also an old wooden chest bound with brass straps. Written on the chest are these words:

BLUE BEARD'S CURSE

IF YOU TAKE MY GOLD
YOU'LL NOT GROW OLD,
BUT FIND YOUR GRAVE
IN BLUE BEARD'S CAVE.

You run outside the cave and yell as loudly as you can. Nick comes running.

Turn to page 24.

You and Nick find a dense grove of trees **41** where you can hide from the pirates. The two of you set to work building a shelter. Later on, Nick gathers firewood while you look for food. You are on your way back with some coconuts when you hear a scream. You peek through the thick brush.

Turn to page 42.

42   The pirates are standing around a man lying on the ground. It's Red Eye! "A scorpion got me," he cries. "I should have paid heed to the curse!"

Suddenly his whole body shakes, and he lies still. Only then do you notice the treasure chest just a few feet away!

"Now there will be more treasure for the rest of us!" says one of the pirates.

"You fool!" says another. "If you touch that **43** chest, the same thing will happen to you!"

The pirates shout and argue. One of them starts to touch the chest but then shrinks back. "Let's get out of here," he says.

You watch the pirates pick up Red Eye's body and start toward the beach.

Turn to page 45.

44   You pick up two handfuls of sand. Just in time! The crocodile is crawling toward you! You throw the sand in its eyes and jump aside. The crocodile thrashes wildly. But it starts toward you again. You throw more sand. Then you run the only way you can—into the water.

The other two crocodiles swim toward you. You have never moved so fast in your life. Alas, not fast enough . . .

The End

You run back to find Nick and lead him to the clearing.

"It's amazing," says Nick. "They were so afraid of the curse that they left the treasure behind!"

"That means it's ours to keep!" you say.

"I guess it does," says Nick, "unless we are afraid of the curse."

"Are you?"

The End

BLUE BEARD'S CURSE
IF YOU TAKE MY GOLD
YOU'LL NOT GROW OLD,
BUT FIND YOUR GRAVE
IN BLUE BEARD'S CAVE.

46   At first it's fun being a pirate. But one day storm clouds appear in the west. The wind begins to blow. The sea turns rough and grey. Huge waves smash against the ship, pitching it wildly up and down. You grab hold of the mast and hang on for your life. You begin to wish you hadn't joined the pirates!

Then you hear men yelling below deck. "We've sprung a leak. Water is pouring in!"

A moment later a giant wave whips the *Caliban* over on its side. Another wave strikes, and then another. The ship plunges beneath the waves, and you and Red Eye and all the other pirates sink to the bottom of the sea.

Glug . . . glug . . . glug.

The End

48   You and Nick hurry back to the cave to hide from the pirates. You sit side-by-side on the treasure chest, staring at the bones and skulls.

You jump from your seat at the sound of a distant roar. Nick runs out of the cave. "It's cannon fire!" he calls. "Come on!"

The two of you run to the top of the hill. From there you can see the *Caliban*'s cannons blazing as it fires at two Navy schooners. Soon there is so much smoke that you can hardly see what's happening. As the smoke clears, the *Caliban* plunges beneath the waves!

"So much for Red Eye and his crew!" you say. "I wonder if any more treasure went to the bottom along with the *Caliban*."

"Yes, but it's too deep there for us to get it," says Nick.

"Maybe not," you say. "Someday, we'll come back and search for that treasure, too!"

Nick grins. "Let's shake on it," he says.

The End

50   The *Caliban* is sinking fast. You start climbing the main mast. Suddenly the water stops rising. The ship has hit bottom, but the masts are still sticking out of the water!

You are able to crawl up into the crow's-nest. From there, you can see that the *Eagle* has anchored nearby. Captain Frye and his first mate, Mr. Pym, are rowing toward you in the whaleboat. In a few minutes they pull alongside. You let go of the mast and jump into the whaleboat.

"You've certainly earned your share of the treasure," says Captain Frye. "Now all we have to do is find it!"

The End

52   You step on the crocodile's back and jump! You claw and pull yourself up onto firm ground. You're safe at last!

As soon as you can get your breath, you start back to the beach. Soon you see Captain Frye, Nick, and Mr. Pym. They come running to meet you!

"Thank goodness you're safe," says Captain Frye. "You should see what we found while we were looking for you!"

He leads you to an old wooden chest. You gasp when you see hundreds of gold coins, rubies, emeralds, and pearls inside!

"What are you going to do with your share of the treasure?" asks Nick.

"Well," you reply, "I guess I'll save it until I grow up. Then I'll buy a ship and go sailing for sunken treasure!"

The End

ABOUT THE AUTHOR

Edward Packard, a graduate of Princeton University and Columbia Law School, practices law in New York City. He developed the unique storytelling approach used in the CHOOSE YOUR OWN ADVENTURE™ series while thinking up bedtime stories for his three children.

ABOUT THE ILLUSTRATOR

Paul Granger is a prize-winning illustrator and painter.

Now you can have your favorite Choose Your Own Adventure® Series in a variety of sizes. Along with the popular pocket size, Bantam has introduced the Choose Your Own Adventure® series in a Skylark edition and also in Hardcover.

Now not only do you get to decide on how you want your adventures to end, you also get to decide on what size you'd like to collect them in.

SKYLARK EDITIONS

☐	15120	The Circus #1 E. Packard	$1.75
☐	15207	The Haunted House #2 R. A. Montgomery	$1.95
☐	15208	Sunken Treasure #3 E. Packard	$1.95
☐	15149	Your Very Own Robot #4 R. A. Montgomery	$1.75
☐	15308	Gorga, The Space Monster #5 E. Packard	$1.95
☐	15309	The Green Slime #6 S. Saunders	$1.95
☐	15195	Help! You're Shrinking #5 E. Packard	$1.95
☐	15201	Indian Trail #8 R. A. Montgomery	$1.95
☐	15191	The Genie In the Bottle #10 J. Razzi	$1.95
☐	15222	The Big Foot Mystery #11 L. Sonberg	$1.95
☐	15223	The Creature From Millers Pond #12 S. Saunders	$1.95

HARDCOVER EDITIONS

☐	05018	Sunken Treasure E. Packard	$6.95
☐	05019	Your Very Own Robot R. A. Montgomery	$6.95
☐	05031	Gorga, The Space Monster #5 E. Packard	$7.95
☐	05032	Green Slime #6 S. Saunders	$7.95

Prices and availability subject to change without notice.

Buy them at your local bookstore or use this handy coupon for ordering: